U0081585

陳明克 著・譯
Poems and translated by Chen Ming-keh

船 塢 裡

In Dock

陳明克漢英雙語詩集
Chinese – English

台灣詩叢 • Taiwan Poetry Series 09

【總序】詩推台灣意象

叢書策劃／李魁賢

　　進入21世紀，台灣詩人更積極走向國際，個人竭盡所能，在詩人朋友熱烈參與支持下，策畫出席過印度、蒙古、古巴、智利、緬甸、孟加拉、馬其頓等國舉辦的國際詩歌節，並編輯《台灣心聲》等多種詩選在各國發行，使台灣詩人心聲透過作品傳佈國際間。接續而來的國際詩歌節邀請愈來愈多，已經有應接不暇的趨向。

　　多年來進行國際詩交流活動最困擾的問題，莫如臨時編輯帶往國外交流的選集，大都應急處理，不但時間緊迫，且選用作品難免會有不週。因此，興起策畫【台灣詩叢】雙語詩系的念頭。若台灣詩人平常就有雙語詩集出版，隨時可以應用，詩作交流與詩人交誼雙管齊下，更具實際成效，對台灣詩的國際交流活動，當更加順利。

　　以【台灣】為名，著眼點當然有鑑於台灣文學在國際間名目不彰，台灣詩人能夠有機會在國際努力開拓空間，非為個人建立知名度，而是為推展台灣意象的整體事功，期待開創台灣文學的長久景象，才能奠定寶貴的歷史意義，台灣文學終必在世界文壇上佔有地位。

　　實際經驗也明顯印證，台灣詩人參與國際詩交流活動，很受重視，帶出去的詩選集也深受歡迎，從近年外國詩人和出版社與本人合作編譯台灣詩選，甚至主動翻譯本人詩集在各國文學雜誌或詩刊發表，進而出版外譯詩集的情況，大為增多，即可充分證明。

　　承蒙秀威資訊科技公司一本支援詩集出版初衷，慨然接受【台灣詩叢】列入編輯計畫，對台灣詩的國際交流，提供推進力量，希望能有更多各種不同外語的雙語詩集出版，形成進軍國際的集結基地。

2017.02.15誌

目次

CONTENTS

老學者

長久以來
他總懷抱無比的信心
經由數學
經由實驗
他要走到上帝的身邊

如今是更接近了
就等著
計算機完成交付的程式
閃閃的螢光
是千萬年來的呼求
他在恍惚的星塵之間
聆聽著神
超乎可解與不可解之間
飄飄茫茫的聲音

他的朋友從獄中回來
跟他訴說
那年的暴動
刺耳的槍聲已經模糊
人影卻不斷分裂、旋轉
他霍然站起
腦海中被酒激發的血，像怒潮
幻化成漫漫長夜
無法捉摸、糾纏不清的呼求

他剛講完課
年輕的學生在窗外
微笑著不停走過
　　不知道什麼時候變成
白茫茫的雨腳
深深踏入春日的稻田
他擱下宇宙生成論

萎頓於無法捉摸的春風之中
　（唯有疲弱的嘆息）

壯年（九一年心情）

我們沿著河岸行走
入秋微涼的風托起高遠的天空
小販蒸熟的菱角香味
在黃昏斑駁的陰影中
輕快地穿梭
精壯之年的我們
不覺相視而笑

我們一路談著茫茫浩浩的宇宙
如何生成如何運作
彷彿在光潔的神的面前
我們穿過飄忽搖曳的陰影
來到耀眼的水銀燈下
在地面急速地刻劃
那美麗的式子

沉默的行人
漸漸埋入黑暗
我們的心情突然沉重起來
彷彿中有人絮絮密商
我們驚恐地尋找
陰影如鬼魂縹緲飛轉
黏身地覆蓋慌亂的人群

我們終於淒涼地笑了起來
手上握著殘破的,要掉落地上的式子
我的朋友說
我像販攤上飽滿的菱角

蒲公英

風，好舒服
困在石縫中的我
因此能夠揮手
期待風吹來花香般的信息
（自虛空之中）

啊！我還在等待
不要把我吹散
我將消失無影

1997.4

貓樣歲月

我聽到貓在窗口
我促狹地對它吼叫
隨手抓球砸向它
它沉靜地蜷曲著身體

我不知道追逐什麼
和朋友，和人
推擠碰撞
呼嘯如醉漢
年少的臉上迷惘而又歡喜
春天的霧像流水
靜靜地在交錯的路上

我抓起研究報告
追趕著貓出去
隨著噪熱的遊行人群

把手中的紙張當作旗幟
揮舞

被驅趕後，我
緊緊捏住殘破的紙
鳳凰花不停地落下
雷電沉悶地響著
厚重的雨水中
彷彿有人幽幽看著我

似夢似醒地交揉著
那長髮少女幽幽的眼神
彷彿風中不定的花香
忽然走近，忽然走遠
我跌坐在研究室雜亂的紙堆
苦苦思索著終極的答案
花香令我苦惱而又歡喜

我尋找著花香
走近窗口（將近下雨的陰暗天色）
我漸漸斑白的頭髮中
那少女燦然地笑著
和同伴很快地走遠
我想叫住貓
它無聲地掠過
像個錯覺

天使之舞

不再甜美
纍纍的稻穗被轉涼的秋風
泛起微波
在破裂的地面來回訴說末日將臨
我勉強來到跪倒的大樓前
唱著聖詩
安慰自帳篷走出的人

昏灰的天色中
他們唱著聖詩
想著世界終結
新天新地浮現
我在搖晃不停的樹葉下
慌亂地徘徊
去或不去

有人坐在廢墟中哭泣
裸露的鋼筋像掙扎的手
自地底伸出
我想走近
警衛吹起刺耳的哨音
塵埃被風吹起
廢墟一片空茫

他們邊唱邊圍著跳舞
一圈一圈訴說滿心的期待
風吹著布條不斷顫抖
我孤單地
恍若迷失在異地

她忽然在跳舞的人群中
甜甜地笑著
他們不斷訴說恩典降臨

她慢慢走向我
歌聲卻驟然終止
人群紛亂如起伏不定的稻浪
我要走向哪裡？
飛揚的塵土一片空茫

1999.10

急雨

雨急急跑來
黑暗緊跟在後
掩蓋了一切
　只剩地面上無數雨珠摔碎
　化成茫茫白霧

雨焦急地找路
終於翻越譁然的屋頂
來到水池邊
一圈圈的水波
是逃逸之門？

2001.6.15

花露

柏油路邊冒出的草
努力地開花
　　想著未來
花瓣上的露珠
是昨晚天使的輕觸

陣陣汽油煙霧搧打花瓣
露珠還留有痕跡
花努力地展開燦爛
不叫有露痕的花瓣掉落

天使傳錯信息？

2001.7.21

小麻雀

行道樹下
小麻雀蹦蹦跳著
尾巴忽高忽低
招引同伴
追尋什麼？

它分得清為什麼不停來回？
離迷的日影
還是飄忽的風

它張著嘴喘氣

2002.5.25

油桐花

為什麼不等我
盛開就掉落
覆蓋灌木叢
如失神的雲
樹叢底下蜥蝪搖搖擺擺
踏著枯葉

可是昨晚花浮起我
花瓣中我看到雲和天空
雪白的橋正在連結
　不知道是用雲還是花
我聽到我等待的腳步聲
急促地從彼端走來

我被汗水濕透
站在飄轉的油桐花外

樹叢下蛇沙沙地遊走
我撿起樹枝揮舞

花不停掉落
腳步聲細細地走來？
　是誰？
我一再壓抑喘息

2003.4.27

暗夜

原以為是小石頭
暗夜直落的雨
我站在門邊
驚訝地發覺被圍困
　　不知道是什麼地方

有隻螢火蟲躲進
稻埕外的樹叢
護著它閃爍的燈火
不斷移動

我拉板凳坐下
做了好多夢
還笑起來呢

啊！這是我的家，台灣

2003.5.15

牽牛花

為了朝露
牽牛花一早就醒來
他漸漸張開的眼睛
閃著晶瑩的朝露無限的未來

朝露忽然不見了
牽牛花到處找
疲憊地在地上爬
眼睛，朝露曾來過，睜不開

2003.6.7

掙來的春天

像門口等待春天的花？
一早要出門的我呆呆望著
今年第一場春雨──歪歪斜斜地糾纏
我一直跨不出腳步
腦海中飛彈曳著火燄穿過夜空
像魔鬼答應的春雨

那麼該向誰祈求？

台北有一群人圍住辦事處
焚燒星條旗
但他們只是罐頭
由另一個強權製造
我們遠遠看著
想起他們渴慕那個強權的呼喊

春雨一下子就停了
短得出奇
我是不是祈禱錯了？
飛彈每天準時在黑暗中呼嘯

花終於開了
辛苦地在花瓣聚集幾滴露珠
春天，艱辛地掙來

2003.9.5於2003印度詩歌節朗誦

小蚱蜢

要跳上天空的小蚱蜢
跳到草尖

不再往上彈跳
這裡的天空最高
它搆不著
總是摔落草叢底下

栽植大樓的地面被風吹得搖晃
但它看到地平線接到天空
它興奮地跳到柏油地面
一腳高一腳低走向天空

喂——！千萬不要跟人問路

2003.11.17

春回

好像昨晚趕路
柏油路邊的小黃花
回來了
帶著影子
迎向微風張開手跳舞

隔壁緊急送醫
好幾天不見的老伯
也笑呵呵回來
越跑越快

鐵門前，他皺緊眉頭
摸不到門把
小黃花牢牢抓緊影子
怕被他搶走
他這才發現

船塢裡
In Dock

匆匆趕路
影子不知丟在那裡

唉呀！春天為什麼也呼喚
死去的人

2004.3.5

草蚊

傍晚出現的草蚊
互相呼喚
不斷搧動薄薄的翅膀
努力地聚在一起

無法抵抗
愈來愈暗的天色
一隻隻飛向燈光

就這樣結束？
地面上一堆
輕飄飄的身體
被忽有忽無的風
吹來吹去

2004.8.11

斑鳩

我從數十封電子郵件找到她
她梳著長髮走到窗邊
眼睛晶亮望著草坪
七十餘隻野雁剛剛飛落
北美的陽光停在紅葉上

我倒看到陽台有幾隻斑鳩
踏著枯葉低頭啄食
風吹得它們羽毛豎起
我輕輕丟出餅乾屑

每天黃昏
斑鳩從天空緩緩劃出
淡淡光芒的弧線
落到陽台
我總急忙離開電腦桌

它們的身軀漸漸改變
來回啄食我丟出的食物

今天天色很快昏暗
窗戶微微搖晃
我靠著窗勉強看到斑鳩
模糊的身影
她從我背後走來
笑著說：野雁吶！
我沒回頭
忍住笑　心裡不斷說
「是斑鳩
被我餵大的斑鳩」
我好想看她驚喜的眼神

但，我不敢回頭
她會在我面前消失

2004.10.27

海浪

一前一後的海浪
一直相伴
卻有無法拉近的距離

天空澄澈的時候
他們都看到天空彎下
截住不斷延伸的世界
「那是終點」他們高興地跳躍
「是天堂？」他們相互凝視

天色變得昏暗
狂風好像要把他們打碎
他們彼此呼喚
不再害怕不斷奔向終點

他們跑上沙灘
卻來不及歡呼

無聲地沒入細沙
一前一後相繼地消失

2005.3.22

臨終

感覺到秋天
山巒上綿延不盡的綠樹
有的突然枯黃

它們這才看到同伴
也看到自己
在掉落之前

2005.1.12

太早

太早開的花
牢牢地抓著樹枝
即使已枯萎

2007.3.22

蒲公英的飛翔

突來的風吹動什麼
黑暗一層層落下
雷聲從遠處奔走過來
我緊緊抓住方向盤
卻也看到柏油路邊
盛開多日的蒲公英
怯怯地展開一團絨毛

我年少時也曾看到
　　從停停走走的公車
雨猛烈敲打車窗
玻璃模糊
我只能看見包圍我
擁擠的潮濕的人群
雨衣雨傘不斷滴水
　　那就是我狹窄的世界

公車突然煞車
不知是誰趴向車窗
我從手印看到窗外
蒲公英花瓣緩緩飄落

我匆匆在校門口下車
蒲公英原本應該飛起的花絮
像一片刮落的絨毛黏在牆腳
鐵線般的雨絲密密麻麻
圍困我
圍牆上的標語仍然腥紅
仍然強迫我們

停停走走的車流中
我小心控制車行的速度
蒲公英等了這麼久
絨毛輕輕顫動

就這麼一次
不要這個時候下雨
讓蒲公英飛起來
從我無法離開的路

2006.4.30

營火

年輕時的某個夜晚
在夢中重現
　存在的果真永遠存在
熟識的人等我走過去

臉孔都被參差的光影覆蓋
說話聲忽遠忽近
無法靠近

我走過搖晃不定的影子
伸出手握住營火

黑暗像布幕掉落
我看不見自己
大聲呼喚　卻沒有聲音
哪一個瞬間真實存在？

2007.2.4

風的生命

困在山谷的風
來回奔跑呼喊
掃動樹葉

衝出山谷的風
嘆息聲中消失
如人最後的嘆息

這樣的風
只存在受困於山谷？
靈魂也是這樣？

2007.7.25

墜落的露珠

清晨路過草地
寂靜得聽見
草擦過我的褲管

突然看到發亮的露珠
輕輕飄落
在我的褲管消失
我感覺到我的死亡

好幸福啊
晶瑩的露珠

2008.6.12

拒馬釘上的花

插在拒馬的玫瑰花
釘子刺進身體
應該很痛吧
生命沒有未來

仍然盛開　毫不縮減
因為相信微風
是天使的輕吻

瑞和人群擠在拒馬前面
汗水擦不掉　流進眼睛
吶喊不承認
躲在拒馬後面的江陳會
「正在談論我們的價格」
瑞氣憤地吼叫

拒馬後面群警如安靜的森林
瑞抬頭再次吶喊
驚訝地看到玫瑰花

輕撫玫瑰花的微風
從哪裡來？
也輕撫瑞的臉龐

2009.1.22

行經木棉樹

夾在人群中走出捷運站
推擠著經過木棉樹下

聽到吱吱喳喳的聲音
盛開的木棉花中
不知道是什麼鳥
跳躍著　樹枝花朵輕晃

總有一兩隻跳到樹梢
張望著　輕輕叫著
戒備遠遠盤旋的鷹

好幸福的鳥雀
敵人不隱藏在同伴中

木棉花重重掉落腳前
是你們送給我的？
我也能長出翅膀？

2009.3.18

雨後

不要割草啦
它們正忙著戴好
上帝的珍珠

2010.7.30

暮蟬

為了不要夜晚
從濃密的樹葉
一隻隻地抓
快要啼叫的暮蟬
關進隔音罐

秋天卻在樹葉
長出來

2010.9.6

蜻蜓

一隻蜻蜓停在
翹起的雨刷
牠寂靜地等待
以為擋風玻璃是水池？

我竟然是牠

2010.9.10

流螢

從黑暗中突然出現
是流螢？飄忽不定
一瞬間熄滅
又將在哪裡出現？

妳的眼睛在我心裡閃亮
尋找我？

我不曾看見我

輸送帶

輸送帶不斷往前捲動
數不清的礦石被帶著走
將被打碎重塑
平穩地嗡嗡鳴叫的是馬達
卻看不見

沒有人問過我
我是誰？

礦石在輸送帶上抖跳
劇烈得彷彿想跳走

我每天準時搭公車
到公司、回家
有一瞬我看到逃走的機會
我以畢生之力跳落

如礦石掉落輸送帶的盡頭
那是什麼地方？

2010.3.28

船塢裡的船

它們望著海？
想些什麼？

它們原本空無
吊車吊起鋼樑鐵板
以烈火焊燒切割
連結成船的瞬間
它們就感覺海的呼喚

我終於明白
血肉構成的我
感覺到超乎肉身的呼喚

能不能再清楚一點？
像船聽見海

2010.10.24

遊民的路上

天空灰濛濛
幾個遊民低頭亂走
　套著塑膠袋
像風吹枯葉的聲音

長長的大馬路
綠燈突然一路亮起來
荷槍的警察擋住遊民
落葉從警察腳下鑽過去

車隊急速奔馳
遊民用力拉
要飛起來的塑膠袋
縮著身體打轉

警車的紅藍燈不斷閃爍尖叫
那個人要去宣導減肥

2011.1.28

人群中

人群中停停走走
擔心跌倒、被踐踏

什麼時候
才能像花叢的花
追著微風

2011.12.7

打不開門

輕輕的腳步聲
在漫長的走廊裡尋找

漸漸走過來
我卻打不開門

2011.12.14

雨之花

雨跑了多遠？
不能開花　卻在地面
撞出一朵朵花

我也正在尋找我的花

2012.4.16

默默看著

黃澄澄的落花
淹沒了整條路
還在掉落

原來不只是我
努力開花的小草
也默默看著

2014.6.8

落花之夢

樹底下陰暗的木桌
花瓣不知掉落
多久了

啊！在做夢呢
拉著照到它的陽光
要跳舞耶

2014.7.29

下午茶

翠蘆莉紛紛掉落

他轉頭
不斷攪拌咖啡

這樣咖啡香
會留住陽光？

2015.10.28

飛向天空

樹葉也忙碌著
在風中搖晃出聲

樹下詩人忙著唸詩

樹葉抓著風
飛到藍天

啊！是一灘水
映著天空和樹

只在水窪中
樹才如此靠近天空
詩人以一寸之氣
吹送詩

2016.9.4於淡水大樹書房

露珠

露珠失神地滑下
沿著彎曲的細枝
將掉落消失

細枝末端
一朵櫻花盛開

2017.3.19

油桐花葉

油桐的葉子
因花而活？

花為掌聲飄落
被輕輕捧起

葉子默默枯黃
掉落　被踩踏
也不大聲叫喊

陽光為什麼
穿越密林
輕撫落葉

2017.12.1

黃昏

麻雀各自飛落
忙著覓食

為一粒米
拍翅尖叫追趕

忽然互相依偎

啊！黃昏

2018.2.17

阿夫林的小孩

那小男孩如往常
要去學校
早晨溫柔的陽光
停留在他細嫩的小臉
他瞇著眼睛
想像春天

那個小男孩
在半路停下來
他聽到隱隱的春雷
他想起他背著槍
離家的哥哥說
「我會為你帶春天
和愛小孩的國
回來
像春天擁抱著樹」

他跑向春天
春雷卻變成炮火
籠罩他
他來不及感覺
春天的擁抱

2018.3.26

花的祈禱

老厝的磚牆縫裡
長出一株草
會像老厝一樣
長久吧

庭院裡面
一朵花
默默祈求直到
掉落

2018.9.24
2018.9.23於石牆仔

雨珠

蜻蜓啊
不要飛那麼快
我要跳落你身上

載我飛翔
我不要落地

2018.9.26

百年

牧師樓前
綠草地的雨珠
怔怔望著
百年紅磚牆

它想落在
紅磚上
感覺什麼是
百年

2018.9.26

露珠 II

「好圓好美啊」

小女孩輕輕
把花瓣上的露珠
彈入手掌

她哭了起來
手掌裡面
只是一灘水

彈飛的露珠
掛在她臉頰？

作者簡介

　　陳明克（生於1956）1986年於清華大學獲得物理博士學位。1987年，加入笠詩社。現在是笠詩刊編委。結集的詩集有十本，中短篇小說集有兩本。獲得七項文學獎。作品探索生命的意義。常以隱喻表現。

In Dock

An Old Taiwanese Scholar

He has long held an unquestioned belief

that through mathematics

and experimentation

he will one day reach God

Now it's getting closer

just waiting

for the computer to finish its program task

on the screen

calls of thousands of years are flashing

in the dim stardusts

he listens to God

above the comprehensible

and incomprehensible sound

His friend, coming out of prison

was telling him about the riot of the fateful year

the piercing gunshots had become blurred

yet the human figures kept disintegrating and whirling

suddenly he rose up

the alcohol-excited blood was rushing into his head

and turning everything into a long, long night

filled with untouchable, tangled calls

He had just finished his lecture

outside the window, endless young students

smiled and passed by

and somehow they turned into dazzlingly white raindrops

planting their feet deeply in the spring fields

he put down the Formation of Universe

and withered away in the imperceptible spring breeze

(only a weary sigh remained)

(Translated by William Marr)

The Prime of Life

We walked along the river
The slightly cool wind held the sky far away
The smell of water chestnuts, streamed by street vendors
circulated nimbly
In the variegated shadows at nightfall
We, in the prime of life
unconsciously looked at each other and smiled

We talked about the vast universe all the way
How to be created, how to be operated
as if we stood before God, bright and clean
We passed through the shadows, swung uncertainly
came closer to the shining mercury lamps
quickly depicted on the ground
those beautiful formulas

船塢裡
In Dock

The silent walkers

were buried gradually into the dark

We felt depressed suddenly

It seemed some were dealing incessantly and secretly

We, scarred, looked for them

Shadows, floated and whirled secretly as ghosts

covered and adhered the tangled crowd

We finally smiled sadly

grasped the broken and falling formulas in our hands

My friend said

it looked like I was a fully mature water chestnut

Taraxacum

The wind, how comfortable is
So I, locked in the crevice of stones,
can wave hands and expect
the wind carries news in flowers smell to me
(from the vast emptiness)

Oh! I am still waiting
Do not blow me to disperse
I shall disappear

Catlike Years

I heard a cat outside the window
I yelled to it spitefully
picked a ball at hand to throw at it
It curled up itself silently

I do not know what I pursued for
In friends, in crowd
we pushed and collided with each other
shouting as drunkards
perplexed but happy, shown on our young faces
Fog in spring was flowing as water
Silently on the cross roads

I grasped my research report
Went out, chased after the cat,
Followed the noisy and passionate marchers,

Brandished the papers in my hand violently
as a flag

After being driven away, I
clutched the broken papers
Flowers of flame trees were falling continually
It thundered as big drums
In the heavy rain
It seemed someone musingly looked at me

I seemed to be in dreams when I waked
Those mused eyes of that long-haired girl
unexpectedly came closer to me and went away
as the smell of flowers in the wind
I fell in disordered papers in my study room
thought the final answer in pains
I was worried but also happy for the smell of flowers

船塢裡
In Dock

I was looking for the smell of flowers

came closer to the window in the dark, when it was going to rain

In my hairs, getting white recently

that girl laughed in full bloom

went faraway with her friends

I wanted to call the cat, not go

It glanced me and passed silently

as my illusion

Dance of Angels

No longer pleasant

clustered rice ears rippled

in the cooling wind of autumn

The cracked earth told over and over of the advent of doomsday

I forced myself to come to the prostrate building

singing the holy songs

to consol those coming out of the tents

Under the gray sky

they sang the holy songs

thinking of the end of the world

and the emergence of a new cosmos

Beneath a tree whose leaves shook incessantly

I paced to and fro bewildered

whether or not to go away

船塢裡
In Dock

Some sat in the ruins weeping
Naked reinforcing rods looked like struggling hands
stretching out of the ground
I tried to go near
the guard gave a piercing whistle
Dust blew up in a wind
across the vast emptiness of ruins

They danced as they sang and went in circles
one ring after another to tell of their heartfelt hope
The wind was blowing strips of cloth in a steady flutter
I felt lonely
as if lost in a foreign land

Suddenly in the group of people dancing
I saw her smiling sweetly
They kept on telling of the grace to come

As she slowly approached me
the singing abruptly stopped
The crowd undulated erratically like waves of rice
Where should I go?
Dust in the air across the vast emptiness

(Translated by K.C. Tu and Robert Backus)

Shower

Rains hurriedly ran

The dark followed close behind

covered up everything

except the raindrops, dashed to pieces on the ground

They became blindly white mists

Rains worriedly looked for ways out

Finally, they passed over the noisy roof

to the bank of a pool

Are the circles of the ripples

the doors, they can escape from?

Dews on Flowers

Grasses that pierced out from the asphalted roadside

Bloom as they can

thinking of the future

Dewdrops on the petals

   were the soft touches by angel last night?

A burst of petrol smog hit the petals

There still leave dew-marks on the petals

The flowers strive to keep in full bloom

for not letting petals with dew-marks to drop down

Did the angel bring the message by mistake?

A Little Sparrow

Under street trees
a little sparrow skipped about
Its tail was lifted up and soon swept down
It called and beckoned its companions

What was it searching for?
Did it know clearly why it came and went without stop?
For the confused shadows in the sun?
Or for the indefinite wind?

It opened its beak to pant

Flowers of Tung Trees

Why not wait for me?
They fell soon after full bloom
covered brushwood
as dejected clouds
Under trees, lizards staggered
stepping on dry leaves

But flowers supported me to float up last night
In flower petals, I saw clouds and the sky
A snow white bridge was being built
with clouds or flowers, I do not know
I heard footsteps, I expected
coming urgently from the other side

I drip with sweats
standing outside the falling and whirling petals

船塢裡
In Dock

Snakes crawl under trees
I pick up a tree branch to brandish

Flowers are falling continuously
Are the slight footsteps coming closer?
Whose?
I suppress my heavy breathing again and again

Dark Night

I thought them as small stones

Rain drops falling heavily in the dark night

I stood by the door

Sensed in surprise that I was besieged

I did not know which place it was

A firefly hid itself

in trees outside the grain-drying square

protecting its flashing lights

It moved constantly

I pulled a bench and sat down

I had many dreams

and even smiled

Oh! Here is my home, Taiwan

Morning Glory

For the morning dew

the morning glory rises very early

His eyes, opening slowly, shines

the unlimited future of the lustrous dew

The morning dew disappears suddenly

The morning glory looks for her everywhere

He is so tired he crawls on the ground

He can not open his eyes, the morning dew ever stayed

Hard-earned Spring

Like the flowers outside the front gate anticipating Spring?
Ready to leave, I, gazed aimlessly
The first Spring shower, crisscrossing entangled
I hesitated to step out
A missile with a fiery tail across the sky flashed in my head
like the Spring shower promised by the devil

Then to whom should I pray?

A crowd surrounded underground US Embassy in Taipei
burning Stars-and-Stripes flags
But they are mere tins
produced by another power
We observed from afar
recalling their longing cries for that power

船塢裡
In Dock

Spring shower passed quickly
Surprisingly brief
Had I said a wrong prayer?
Missiles screeched in the dark on time nightly

The flowers bloomed at last
assiduously gathering a few dews amongst the petals
Spring, won the day painstakingly

A Little Grasshopper

A little grasshopper, which wants to jump to the sky,
jumps to the tip of grass

It never jump again
The sky over it is the highest
It could not touch even jumping
It always fell to the bottom of underbrush

The ground, planted with big buildings,
is blown to swing and sway by the wind
But it finds the horizon touches the sky
It excitedly jumps to the asphalted ground
walks to the sky as it is on swaying grasses

Hey-! extremely not to ask human about how to go

Spring Comes Back

The yellow flowers, at the asphalted way side

seemed to run hurriedly last night

They come back

with their shadows

They face the breeze, open their arms and dance

The old man, my neighbor, emergently sent to hospital

several days ago,

also comes back and cackles

He runs faster and faster

Before the iron door, he knits his eyebrows tightly

He can not touch the door knob

The yellow flowers hold their shadows closely

for not to be rent by him

At this moment, he is aware

in his hurry run,
he lost his shadow

Ai! Why spring also calls
the dead

Grass Mosquitoes

Grass mosquitoes, appeared in the late afternoon
called each other
flapped their thin wings without stop
They strived hard to gather together

They could not stand against
the darker and darker color of sky
They flew to lamplight one by one

So, is it over?
On the ground, a pile of
bodies, floating as dust
were blew by the wind, which suddenly appeared and disappeared
to here and there

Turtledoves

I found her from several dozen E-mails

She was combing her long hair and went to the window

Her eyes, looking at lawns, were brilliant and bright

More than 70 wild geese flew and fell just now

The sunshine in North America stopped on the maple leaves

While I saw several turtledoves in the balcony

bowing and pecking when stepping on the dead leaves

The wind blew so that their feathers were held up

I threw out biscuit bits gently

At every nightfall

after slowly marking in the sky

arc of the thin brilliant rays

turtledoves fell to the balcony

I always left the computer desk in a hurry

Their bodies had changed gradually

They pecked at the food that I threw out back and forth

It became dim quickly today

The window was shaking slightly

By the window, I saw turtledoves reluctantly

in a blur

She was coming up from behind me

and said with a smile: Wild geese!

I did not turn round

resisting not to smile, said constantly in my heart

'Turtledoves

the turtledoves, which were fed to grow up by me"

I really wanted to see her pleasantly surprised expression in her eyes

However, I did not dare to turn round

for she would disappear in front of me

Waves

The successive waves
were accompanied by each other all the time
But they couldn't make closer.

When the sky was transparent
they all found the sky was curved down
to stop the world that is extending constantly
'That is the terminal point', they jumped cheerfully
'Paradise?' they stared each other.

It became dim
It seemed that the blast broke them
They called each other
No longer in fear
they marched on towards terminal point constantly.

船塢裡
In Dock

They ran on the sandy beach
but had no enough time to hail
They submerged the fine sand silently
and disappeared in succession.

Near the End

Feeling autumn
some of the green trees,
growing on the unlimited chain of mountains,
unexpectedly became withered and yellow

Hence, never before
they found out their companions,
found out themselves too
when they were going to drop

Too Early

In bloom too early

A flower grasped the branch firmly

Even when it dropped

The Flight of the Dandelion

A sudden gust blows

As layers of darkness slowly fall

And roaring thunder approaches fast from the distance

I grip the steering wheel tightly

But can't help noticing dandelions by the roadside

That have been flowering for many days

Coyly displaying their downy parachute balls

When I was young I saw

   from the windows of a bus in stop-and-go traffic

The rain splashing against the panes with force

Glass blurry

All I could make out were the people in the crowded bus

Surrounding me on all sides, wet and soggy

Raincoats and umbrellas dripping without cease

   in my narrowly confined world

Suddenly the bus stopped

Someone was hurled against a window

And through the impression of his hands, outside the window I saw

Dandelion petals gently floating down

At the school gate, I got off in a hurry

The dandelion flakes that should have been swirling through the air

Were instead stuck to the foot of a wall like scraped-off lint

The rain kept falling like dense streams of wire

Hemming me in on all sides

The crimson slogans on the encircling wall

Still threatening us

In the stop-and-go traffic

I drive on, carefully controlling the speed of the car

They have waited for so long, the dandelions

Their downy parachutes trembling ever so lightly

Just for once

Please don't start to rain right now

And let the dandelions fly

Fly away from this road that I can't leave

(translated by David van der Peet 范德培)

Campfire

A certain night, when I was young
reappeared in my dream
What ever existed really exist forever!
Those who knew me well waited for me to go over

Their faces were all covered by mixed shadows and light
The voice of talk was suddenly far, suddenly near
It was unable to go closer

I passed by the shaking shadows
stretched out my hands to hold the campfire

It became dark suddenly as a cloth curtain dropped
I could not see myself
I called loudly, but it was quiet
Which moment existed really?

Life of the Wind

The wind, stranded in the valley
runs and shouts back and forth
and sweeps leaves

It rushes out from the valley
disappearing soon in sighing
as men's last sigh

Thus, does the wind exit
only when it is stranded in valley?

So is the soul?

Falling Dewdrops

Walking in the meadow in early morning

So quiet as to hear

The grass was wiping my trousers

Suddenly I saw shiny dewdrops

Descending slowly

Disappeared on my trousers

I felt my death

How wonderful

as the sparkling and crystal-clear dewdrops

Flowers on the Roadblocks

The roses on the roadblocks
were speared into by nails
It should be very painful
Living with no future

They were in full bloom with no reducing
Because they believed the gentle breezes
 were the angel's soft kisses

Ray and the crowd crowded in front of roadblocks
They could not wipe sweat off, flowing into eyes
They shouted loudly and did not admit
Jiang-chen meeting, hiding behind roadblocks
"They are dealing our price"
Ray roared angrily

船塢裡
In Dock

Policemen were standing behind roadblocks quietly as a forest

Ray looked up and shouted loudly again

He found roses in surprise

Soft breezes dabbed roses

Where it come?

Did it also dab Ray's face ?

Pass Through the Silk Cotton Tree

I went out from the subway station in the crowds
Jostling pedestrians, I walked under the silk cotton trees

I heard creak
What birds were in
the full bloomed kapok flowers?
They were jumping, the branches
and flowers were shaking lightly

Always a few birds jumped to the tree-top
looking around and calling gently
to guard the hawk which was far wheeling

How happy the birds
No enemies hid themselves among the companions

船塢裡
In Dock

A kapok flower fell around my feet heavily

Did the birds gave it to me?

Could I grow wings too?

After Rain

Don't cut the grasses
They were busy in wearing
God's pearls

Evening Cicadas

To stop evening cicadas calling

the night to fall

I, one by one from the thick leaves

catch the evening cicadas

which will yell soon

and shut them in the sound-insulated pot.

However, autumn comes out

from the fading leaves

Dragonfly

A dragonfly stays at
the rain wash which turns upwards
It silently waits for
thinking the windshield is a basin?

Unexpectedly, I am the dragonfly

Firefly Flows

What appear unexpectedly from the darkness?

The firefly flows? Floating here and there

Go out in a flash

Where to appear?

Your eyes are glittering in my heart

Looking for me?

I never saw me

Conveyor

The conveyor belt is scrolled forward constantly
Countless ores are carried to move
And broken to pieces to be reshaped
It is a motor, unseen, tweets droningly and
stably

None ever asked me
who I am

Ores are shaking on the conveyor belt
fiercely as if they want to jump off

I take the bus on time every day
to work and go home
For a moment, I find the opportunity to escape
By all I can, I jump off

As ores fall at the end of the conveyor belt

Where is it?

The Ships in Dock

Are they looking at the sea?
What do they think?

They are nothing originally
The cranes sling the steel girders and sheets
which are then welded and cut by the raging fire
At the moment they are linked up to be ships
they feel the sea is calling

Finally, I understand
Why I, made of flesh and blood,
feel the immortal calling

Can it be a little bit clearer ?
as the ships hear the sea

Vagrants in the Road

Under the gloomy sky
a few vagrants, bending their heads
and wearing plastic bags, wandered
sounded like withered leaves in the wind

In the long road
green lamps suddenly lit up all the way
With rifles, policemen blocked vagrants
Leaves passed through from the legs of policemen

The motorcade fleeted away
Vagrants tugged their plastic bags
not to fly away
Their bowed bodies were spinning

The alert lamps of the police patrol cars flashed and screamed
That man was going to advocate weight loss

In the Crowd

Staggering in the crowd
I worried about falling down, being trampled

When could I,
as a flower in flowers,
catch the breeze

I Couldn't Open the Door

The footsteps sounded soft
looking for me in the long corridor

And gradually coming closer
while I couldn't open the door

Flowers of the Rain

How far the rain ran?

They can't be in blossom

They knocked the ground to be flowers

I'm also looking for my flower

Watch Silently

The fallen yellow flowers
flooded the whole road
Flowers were still falling

Ah! Not only I but
the grasses, striving to be in blossom,
also watch silently

A Fallen Flower's Dream

In the shadow of trees
on the wooden table
how long have the flower
fallen down?

Ah! It was dreaming
It pulled the sunshine on it
to dance

Coffee Break

Flowers were falling

He turned around and
stirred coffee constantly

So that coffee was fragrant enough
to keep the sun?

Fly to the Sky

Leaves were also busy
shaking in the wind
and speaking softly

Poets were busy reading poems

Leaves clung to the wind
to fly to the blue sky

Ah! It is a small puddle
reflecting the sky and the trees

Only in the puddle
the trees are so close to the sky
Poets blew poems
by an inch of breath

Dewdrop

A dewdrop absent-mindedly fell down

Along the curved twigs

it would drop and disappear

At the thin end

a cherry blossom fully bloomed

The Flowers and Leaves of Tung trees

The leaves of Tung trees
live for flowers?

Flowers fade for applause
held softly in hands

Leaves turn brown silently
and fall down
When being stamped, they do not
shut either

For what does sunshine
pass through the dense trees
to softly touch the fallen leaves?

Twilight

Respectively, sparrows fly down
busy looking for food

For a grain of rice
flapping wings
they scream to expel each other

Suddenly they snuggle together

Oh! Twilight

Afrin Boy

As usual that boy wants to
go to school
The tender sunlight in morning
stays in his delicate little face
He blinks and
imagines spring

That little boy
stops on the way
He hears spring thunders faintly
His elder brother with a gun, he recalls
when leaving home, said
"I will bring spring and
a nation which loves and
embraces children as spring
back for you"

船塢裡
In Dock

He runs to spring

but spring thunders become

gunfire and envelop him

There's not enough time for him

to feel the embrace of spring

The Prayer

Among the bricks of the old wall
a grass has grown out
Oh! It will be alive
as long as the old building

In the garden, a flower, staring that grass
silently prays until
it fades

Raindrops

Oh! Dragonfly

Don't fly so fast

I want to jump to your back

Carry me flying

I do not want to land

One Century

In front of Pastor's building
raindrops on green grasses
are blankly looking at
the hundred- year red brick wall

They want to fall
on red bricks
to feel what is
one century

Dewdrops II

"So round and so beautiful"

A little girl softly flips
the dews on the petals
into her palm

She cries
for there is just a pool of water
inside her palm

Are they the dews, flied to
hang on her cheeks?

About the Author

Chen Ming-keh(b. 1956 in Taiwan). He received a PhD in physics from Nat'l Tsing Hua University in 1986. He is now a Professor of the department of Phys., Nat, l Chung-Hsing University. In 1987, he became a member of Li poetry society. He is now a member of editorial broad of Li poetry. His publication includes ten collected poems, and two collected short stories. He was awarded seven prizes of literature in Taiwan. He explored the meaning of life. Metaphors are frequently expressed in his poems.

CONTENTS

語言文學類　PG2254　台灣詩叢09

船塢裡 In Dock
——陳明克漢英雙語詩集

作　　　者 / 陳明克（Chen Ming-keh）
譯　　　者 / 陳明克（Chen Ming-keh）
叢 書 策 劃 / 李魁賢（Lee Kuei-shien）
責 任 編 輯 / 林昕平
圖 文 排 版 / 周妤靜
封 面 設 計 / 楊廣榕

發 行 人 / 宋政坤
法 律 顧 問 / 毛國樑　律師
出 版 發 行 / 秀威資訊科技股份有限公司
　　　　　　114台北市內湖區瑞光路76巷65號1樓
　　　　　　電話：+886-2-2796-3638　傳真：+886-2-2796-1377
　　　　　　http://www.showwe.com.tw
劃 撥 帳 號 / 19563868　戶名：秀威資訊科技股份有限公司
　　　　　　讀者服務信箱：service@showwe.com.tw
展 售 門 市 / 國家書店（松江門市）
　　　　　　104台北市中山區松江路209號1樓
　　　　　　電話：+886-2-2518-0207　傳真：+886-2-2518-0778
網 路 訂 購 / 秀威網路書店：https://store.showwe.tw
　　　　　　國家網路書店：https://www.govbooks.com.tw

2019年8月　BOD一版
定價：200元
版權所有　翻印必究
本書如有缺頁、破損或裝訂錯誤，請寄回更換

國家圖書館出版品預行編目

船塢裡In Dock：陳明克漢英雙語詩集 / 陳明克著. 陳明克
譯 -- 一版. -- 臺北市：秀威資訊科技, 2019.08
　　面；　公分. -- (語言文學類. 台灣詩叢；9)
BOD版
ISBN 978-986-326-715-7(平裝)

863.51　　　　　　　　　　　　　　108011057

讀者回函卡

感謝您購買本書，為提升服務品質，請填妥以下資料，將讀者回函卡直接寄回或傳真本公司，收到您的寶貴意見後，我們會收藏記錄及檢討，謝謝！
如您需要了解本公司最新出版書目、購書優惠或企劃活動，歡迎您上網查詢或下載相關資料：http:// www.showwe.com.tw

您購買的書名：＿＿＿＿＿＿＿＿＿＿＿＿＿＿＿＿＿＿＿＿＿＿

出生日期：＿＿＿＿＿年＿＿＿＿＿月＿＿＿＿日

學歷：□高中 (含) 以下　　□大專　　□研究所 (含) 以上

職業：□製造業　□金融業　□資訊業　□軍警　□傳播業　□自由業
　　　□服務業　□公務員　□教職　　□學生　□家管　　□其它＿＿＿

購書地點：□網路書店　□實體書店　□書展　□郵購　□贈閱　□其他

您從何得知本書的消息？

　□網路書店　□實體書店　□網路搜尋　□電子報　□書訊　□雜誌
　□傳播媒體　□親友推薦　□網站推薦　□部落格　□其他＿＿＿＿＿

您對本書的評價：(請填代號　1.非常滿意　2.滿意　3.尚可　4.再改進)

　封面設計＿＿＿　版面編排＿＿＿　內容＿＿＿　文／譯筆＿＿＿　價格＿＿＿

讀完書後您覺得：

　□很有收穫　□有收穫　□收穫不多　□沒收穫

對我們的建議：＿＿＿＿＿＿＿＿＿＿＿＿＿＿＿＿＿＿＿＿＿＿

＿＿＿＿＿＿＿＿＿＿＿＿＿＿＿＿＿＿＿＿＿＿＿＿＿＿＿＿＿＿

＿＿＿＿＿＿＿＿＿＿＿＿＿＿＿＿＿＿＿＿＿＿＿＿＿＿＿＿＿＿

＿＿＿＿＿＿＿＿＿＿＿＿＿＿＿＿＿＿＿＿＿＿＿＿＿＿＿＿＿＿

11466
台北市內湖區瑞光路 76 巷 65 號 1 樓

秀威資訊科技股份有限公司　　　收

BOD 數位出版事業部

....

（請沿線對折寄回，謝謝！）

姓　　名：＿＿＿＿＿＿＿＿＿　年齡：＿＿＿＿　性別：□女　□男

郵遞區號：□□□□□

地　　址：＿＿＿＿＿＿＿＿＿＿＿＿＿＿＿＿＿＿＿＿＿

聯絡電話：(日) ＿＿＿＿＿＿＿＿＿　(夜) ＿＿＿＿＿＿＿＿＿

E-mail：＿＿＿＿＿＿＿＿＿＿＿＿＿＿＿＿＿＿＿＿＿